Smriti Prasadam-Halls

Alison Brown

KU-418-226

I'll Never Let You Go

BLOOMSBURY

LONDON OXFORD NEW YORK NEW DELHI SYDNEY

Bromley Libraries

30128 80241 158 0

For Smitha, my amazing sister, who is always
there for all of us, with all my love - S.P-H.

For all the grandparents - A.B.

Bloomsbury Publishing, London, Oxford, New York, New Delhi and Sydney

First published in Great Britain in 2016 by Bloomsbury Publishing Plc
50 Bedford Square, London, WC1B 3DP

Text copyright © Smriti Prasadam-Halls 2015
Inspired by Isaiah 41:10 & 43:1-3
Illustration copyright © Alison Brown 2015
The moral rights of the author and illustrator have been asserted

All rights reserved
No part of this publication may be reproduced or transmitted by any means,
electronic, mechanical, photocopying or otherwise,
without the prior permission of the publisher

A CIP catalogue record for this book is available from the British Library

ISBN 978 1 4088 3900 3 (HB)
ISBN 978 1 4088 3901 0 (PB)
ISBN 978 1 4088 3899 0 (eBook)

Printed in China by Leo Paper Products, Heshan, Guangdong

1 3 5 7 9 10 8 6 4 2

All papers used by Bloomsbury Publishing are natural, recyclable products
made from wood grown in well-managed forests.
The manufacturing processes conform to the environmental regulations of the country of origin

www.bloomsbury.com

BLOOMSBURY is a registered trademark of Bloomsbury Publishing Plc

When you are happy,
I hear you sing . . .

. . . you swoop and you soar,

you LOVE everything.

When you are naughty I see that, too . . .

But I know that *really* you know what to do.

When you are bothered and all in a flap,
I wait by your side while you snip and you snap.

When you're excited the world joins with you,

you bounce all about – look I'm bouncing, too!

When you are sad and troubled with fears,
I hold you close and dry all your tears.

When you are sleeping, curled up so tight,
I stay awake, keeping watch through the night.

When you are quiet, I think with you,

I help you find answers, work out what to do.

When you are brave, I'm at your side,
and every adventure we'll take in our stride.

When you aren't sure, you'll feel me near.
When you are scared, I will be here.

For when you are high and when you are low,

I'll be holding you tight . . .

. . . and I'll never let go.